Books by Candy Guard

Turning to Jelly

Jelly Has a Wobble

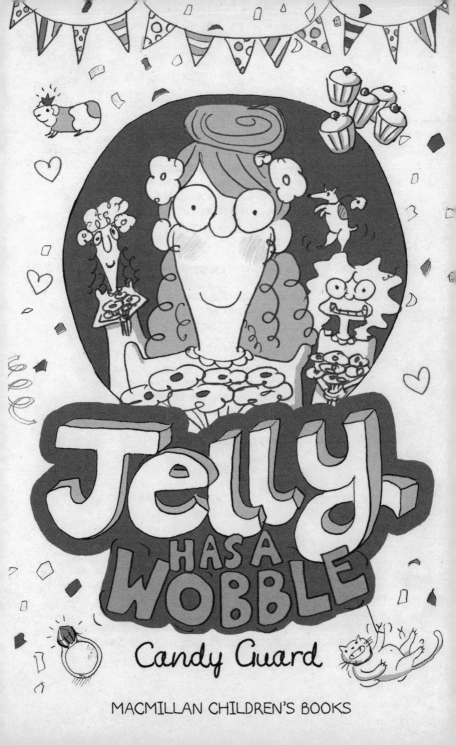

Jelly

HAS A WOBBLE

Candy Guard

MACMILLAN CHILDREN'S BOOKS

FIRST PUBLISHED 2015 BY MACMILLAN CHILDREN'S BOOKS
AN IMPRINT OF PAN MACMILLAN
A DIVISION OF MACMILLAN PUBLISHERS LIMITED
20 NEW WHARF ROAD, LONDON N1 9RR
ASSOCIATED COMPANIES THROUGHOUT THE WORLD
WWW.PANMACMILLAN.COM

ISBN 978-1-4472-5613-7

1 3 5 7 9 8 6 4 2

A CIP CATALOGUE RECORD FOR THIS BOOK IS AVAILABLE FROM
THE BRITISH LIBRARY.

PRINTED AND BOUND BY CPI GROUP (UK) LTD, CROYDON CR0 4YY

For Robin

-1-
Wedding Jells

Remember how I told you my mum L♥VES **PARTIES!** and quite likes her boyfriend, Julian? Well she's thought of the BEST excuse for a party EVER!

She and Julian are getting married! It's a leap year, so <u>SHE</u> asked <u>HIM</u>.

He tried to get out of it.

I don't mind getting married as long as I don't have to be there.

Would a cardboard cut-out of me do? No one will be able to tell the difference.

Mum was **flummoxed** for a moment.
Then she S-l-o-w-l-y started to
take offence.

It wasn't the most **romantic** of proposals or acceptances but Mum was satisfied and immediately started doing the table plan . . .

. . . forgetting to include Julian.

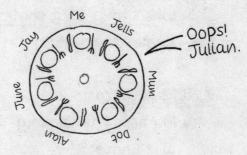

Oops!
Julian.

It was Mum's **fourth** marriage so it obviously wasn't going to be a big posh affair with a meringue dress, a GIANT cake and **embarrassing** speeches. Just something small and informal . . .

AS IF !!!?*?!?

She wanted six bridesmaids to suit her shades-of-summer colour scheme.

They were going to be:

* Me
* Mum's annoying friend's annoying daughter Brittainee from L.A.
* Annoying Cousin Amelia, who's only 8 but thinks she knows everything

And in desperation:

* My best friends, Myf and Roobs
* Cat

Fatty the dog and Ricky from next door were going to be pageboys, and Fatty was also the ring bearer.

(Yes, you can get cat and dog wedding outfits. If you don't believe me, look on eBay.)

My annoying older brother Jay is going to be best man, and his friends — Jock, Brendan and Roger (my ex-crush) — ushers. (Obviously, I was only cheered up for a nanosecond regarding Roger's involvement — he would be bound to see me looking my **worst – again**.)

Myf and Roobs were 'shaking' with excitement, Julian with naked FEAR and Jay with repressed rage about being best man.

I already couldn't take any more! And I'd only known for 2 minutes and 6 seconds.

Annoying Brittainee

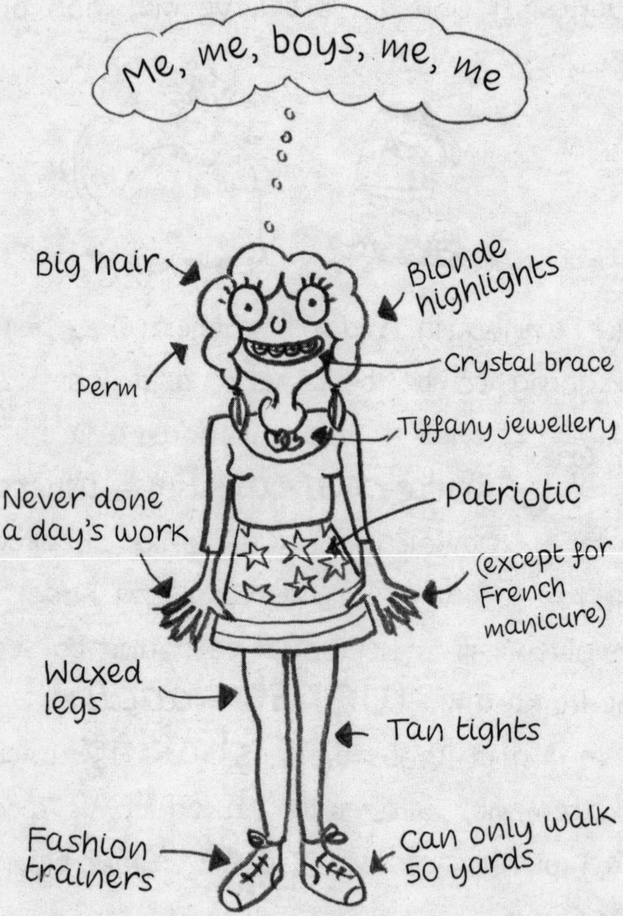

Me, me, boys, me, me

Big hair

Blonde highlights

Perm

Crystal brace

Tiffany jewellery

Never done a day's work

Patriotic

(except for French manicure)

Waxed legs

Tan tights

Fashion trainers

Can only walk 50 yards

Annoying Cousin Amelia

Very brainy

Very honest (rude)

Mandarin

Quantum physics

Me

Military history

Capital cities

Me

Violin symphonies

Russian literature

Me

Latin verbs

Piano grade 8

Stocks and shares

Me 3694.4 + 89.6

Pure Maths

Greek history

Me

Good at ballet →

← Painful feet in adulthood (ha, ha, ha!)

Stupid Ideas

I met Myf and Roobs in the ~Faithful Club~ shed in my back garden. We have been members of the **Faithful Club** since primary school but now we are at Big School it has become more of a <u>secret</u> 𝒞𝓛𝒰𝓑 to avoid any accusations of **immaturity**.

Ricky Chin from next door is our only boy member, and had obviously already forgotten about the meeting. Instead he was in the garden torturing Fatty (who considers himself to be Ricky's BFF) with a digestive biscuit. A fine pair of pageboys *they'll* make.

Myf and Roobs were VERY ᴇˣᶜᴵᵀᴱᴰ about being bridesmaids because they had never been bridesmaids before........

Whereas I had °°°°°°°°°°°°°° three times.

I let them get it out of their systems before
we got down to the **serious** business of the
day . . .

How to raise enough money
to get tickets to see O.M.G.!

O.M.G.! are our FAVOURITE band.
Even Ricky (secretly) likes them
and they are going on TOUR
this year!!

The members are:

Keyboards and lead singer – **Buster Bauble**
(who Myf and I not-so-secretly fancy)

Lead guitar – **Archie Triumph**

Bass – **Dizzy Deakins**

Drums – **Jaz Jenkins**

Jaz Jenkins is the ugly one who Roobs
fancies, because she did a mathematical
equation to work out which one she has the
greatest chance of marrying →
using information gatherered
on their website........

```
┌─────────────────────────────────────┐
│              JAZ JENKINS             │
│          Twitter followers: 3        │
│              Height: 4'9"            │
│             Weight: 7 stone          │
│                Age: 17               │
│   Interests: Maths, computers, Manga │
└─────────────────────────────────────┘
```

 We play their album
We ♥ O.M.G.! continuously.

Right, OK, ideas to make money.

Last meeting we said:

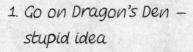

1. Go on Dragon's Den —
   stupid idea
2. Buy a shop — totally stupid
3. Rent out shed — bit stupid
4. Have fete — slightly less
   stupid, but still stupid
5. Beauty parlour, cleaning
   service, put on musical in
   West End . . .

STUPID, STUPID, STUPID.

Roobs said,

But they were all YOUR ideas, Jelly.

And Myf said,

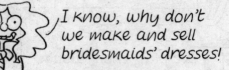

I know, why don't we make and sell bridesmaids' dresses!

And they were off.

Da, da, da, daah . . .

No! like this. Right step, stand, left step, stand.

Stupid

Eventually I gave them crisps and they settled down, but then we just stared at the poster for the O.M.G.! tour in a crisp TRANCE.

Fatty was **barking** outside, having smelt the hydrogenated fat . . .

ROW, row!

. . . and Ricky and Fatty came in and stared at the crisps. Fatty was doing his lazy begging.

'I know!' Ricky said. 'You could enter Fatty for dog shows!'

'Don't be **Silly**,' I said. 'Look at him.'

Myf said, 'Yeah! We can enter him for the Fattest, Ugliest, Most-Badliest Behaved Dog section!'

Myf and Roobs **LAUGHED**.

Tee hee hee

'Do you mind? Only I am allowed to insult Fatty. And anyway he isn't fat.'

'So why's he called 'Fa—'' Myf began, but then she remembered that they were MY crisps and didn't finish her sentence.

Roobs said,

What about a zoo?

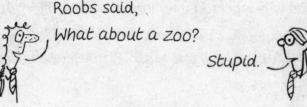

Stupid.

Why d'you keep saying everything's stupid, Jelly?

Why d'you think, Stupid?

Well, I think it's a good idea . . . Stupid!

Yes, Jelly. I mean you've got loads of animals **and** a garden. Come on! I'll do the flyers, we can charge entrance, do tea and cake—

Hold on! I haven't got ZOO animals!

No, but they are all quite unusual, Jelly.

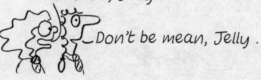

Don't be mean, Jelly . . .

(This is the person who writes every penny you owe her on a chart at the back of her homework book.)

'Yes, Jelly,' said Myf. 'You've got

Fatty

Cat

Guinness

Blossom

Hamwich

Pearl and Dean

Fishcake . . . and what was the one with the long ears?'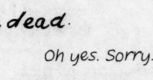

dead.

Oh yes. Sorry.

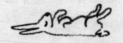

Just then my brother Jay and his mates came in. 'Seen the football, girls?'

GET OUT!

 I said with an **UGLY** expression before seeing my ex-crush, Roger Lovely.

Hi, Roger

Stop showing off, Jelly.

 I'm not!

I said, going **crimson**. Roger winked at me,

Alright, Jells?

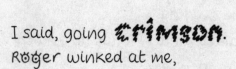

 Myf and Roobs went into (hysterics), like they always do when my brother Jay is around.

'He, he, he, hello Jay,' Myf tittered. 'We're going to have a zoo with all Jelly's pets to raise money for the **O.M.G.!** concert!'

'What a stupid idea,' Jay sneered.

'I know,' I said, unusually agreeing with Jay.

'Well I think it's a great idea, very enterprising,' Röger said.

'It was **my** idea, Röger!' Myf squealed.

'Let me know when it is, and I'll bring my little sister Dilly.'

'Stupid if you ask me,' Jay said. 'But if you're thinking of using the locusts I want a cut. Come on, Rog.'

As they walked away I leapt up and threw the window open —

It was MY idea, Röger!

I could hardly change my mind about the zoo now, without looking like (more of) a **fool**, so I asked my mum if it was OK.

Mum, can we have a zoo in the garden?

A what?

(She was on eBay looking at 'cat couture'.)

A zoo with all our pets.

If they're still alive . . . didn't that one with the long ears die?

If you mean Floppy, yes,

I said, fighting back the tears.

Shame, he'd've looked good in a tiara.

(Mum wasn't very sentimental about animals.)

We voted on the zoo and all said 'aye' and agreed to have it in THREE WEEKS.

-3-
Street Prance

Mum has made me head bridesmaid to try and con me into thinking I am an *extra* **special** bridesmaid but I know it means I have to organise everything like the hen night, the bridesmaids and the **flowers**, have my shoulder ·cried· on and generally be bossed about. This of course should be the job of the bride's mother, but for reasons that will soon become clear, Mum hasn't told her yet.

Mum got us all together and showed us a wedding on YouTube where the bridesmaids enter the church doing a street dance followed by the bride miming to a famous R'n'B song and every-one is **REALLY** impressed.

Don't tell me you're expecting us to do that?

Why not?

None of us can street dance.

So? Oh please, Jells.

Mum's eyes went watery and she started to get that *wild* look. Jay muttered to me,

She's gonna blow — you'd better agree.

I . . .

But then Myf, ever the optimist, said,

There're street-dancing classes starting tomorrow twice a week after school, I think we should go.

I had to admit that I did quite *fancy* learning street dance, and we had decided that we **should** do an after-school thing. It was better than Myf's other suggestion of doing taxidermy (she'd seemed a bit too interested in whether Floppy had been buried or cremated) or Roob's suggestion of doing morris dancing with Mr Bucket.

(Judging by her maraca-playing incident at orchestra, she'd be a danger to society with those sticks.)

So the next day we got the bus to the street-dance class. Melanie the teacher just stood at the front with her back to us and expected us to follow her moves. Myf threw herself into it . . .

23

but Roobs and I just couldn't do it — we
seemed unable to pⁱᶜₖ both feet up off
the ground at the same time without
falling over.

Roobs cricked
her neck doing a
forward roll . . .

and I did a handstand
which didn't involve
my hands or standing.

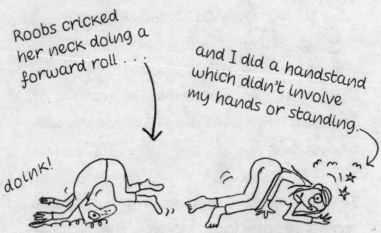

doink!

Melanie said we'd all done REALLY well,
even though she hadn't watched us, and
Roobs and I decided to believe her.

The next class was a :nightmare:
— we all had to run and throw
ourselves into a cartwheel
halfway across the room
and then keep _r_u_n_n_i_n_g_.
When it came to my turn I
ran very **fast** and just kept
running and hoped no one noticed I didn't
do a cartwheel. Roobs ran daintily into
the middle, crouched down
with her hands on the floor,
jumped her feet an inch
off the ground and then
continued daintily running.

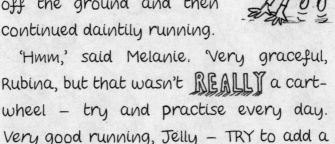

'Hmm,' said Melanie. 'Very graceful,
Rubina, but that wasn't **REALLY** a cartwheel — try and practise every day.
Very good running, Jelly — TRY to add a
cartwheel next time.'

-4-
Toast Addicts

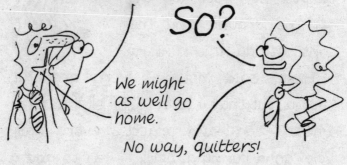

The next time there was a class we waited at the bus stop for 25 minutes. Roobs kept saying the bus route was **obviously** non-operational, because there was **supposed** to be one every 15 minutes.

Come on, Myf, we'll be too late now.

SO?

We might as well go home.

No way, quitters!

Like with all after-school activities Roobs and I started hoping for an excuse not to have to go. We started praying the bus wouldn't come. We'd gone right off the **WHOLE** idea.

Right, one more minute,
then we're going . . .

3 seconds passed

1 Mississippi, 2 Mississippi, 3 Mississippi

Right, we're going!

Roobs and I said, and ~~dashed~~ off.

27

Myf, on the other hand, though untalented at most things, is very good at being Patient and **DETERMINED** and continued to wait.

The bus is coming!!

YOU TWO!!!

What did she say?

No idea!

Once you've decided not to do something you don't want to do, there's **NO GOING BACK**.

Roobs and I felt like naughty school girls (probably because we **were** naughty school girls) as we made our way back to mine,

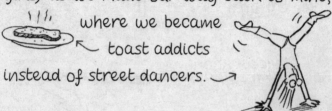

where we became toast addicts

instead of street dancers. ➔

There was a **WHOLE** LOAF of
white bread on the sideboard a[nd I]
started with just one slice, but it w[as] so
delicious . . .

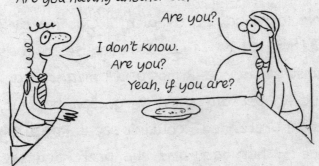

Are you having another bit?

Are you?

I don't know.
Are you?

Yeah, if you are?

(It reminded me of Mum and Julian
egging each other on to watch more
and more episodes of their DVD box sets.)

We continued like this until . . .

Jelleee! Roooobs!
I've just bought that loaf!

cat Napper

We were having a Faithful Club meeting in the shed. Myf was late because she was at street dance. Roobs and I **meant** to go, but Roobs said she'd forgotten her kit, and I pretended I couldn't see it **peeping** out of her bag, and she pretended she couldn't see me pretending etc. etc.

'Oh no,' I said in a faux-disappointed voice. I can't go if you're not going. It's not fair on you. Shall we go back to mine and eat toast?

I suppose so . . .

. . . Roobs said in an equally unconvincing disappointed voice.

30

Then we hurried away before Myf could see us, barely able to suppress our squeals of excitement. I even saw some **dribble** escape from DRIBBLE the corner of Roobs' mouth.

On slice of toast number seven which we had snuck to the shed, we heard Myf's voice before we saw her.

'Oi, you two! Look what I can do!!'
Then she **back** F^LI^{PP}E_D into the shed.

Mind my toast!

WOO!

'You two really should have kept on coming! It's great!' Myf enthused.

We watched Myf flipping all over the garden.

Roobs said, 'I wish we'd kept going now.'

'We'd be able to do that if we had,' I agreed.

Roobs sighed, 'Too late now . . . are you having another bit of toast?'

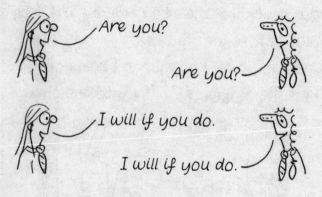

Are you?

Are you?

I will if you do.

I will if you do.

For goodness sake shut up, you two!

Myf yelled.

Let's start the meeting!

Roobs had done the flyers for the zoo

on her Dad's computer. Myf had drawn
a terrible picture of an elephant and a
terrible picture of a giraffe to attract the
crowds. Our job for today was to deliver
them round the neighbourhood.

PRIVATE ZOO

(NO GIRAFFES)

LOTS OF UNUSUAL AND EXOTIC ANIMALS.

ADMISSION FEE 2 POUNDS

REFRESHMENTS AVAILABLE (NOT FREE)

22 RIDGEWELL ST.

2 - 5 P.M. SAT 6 MAY

(. . . OR ELEPHANTS)

We delivered them round the block but
weren't sure whether to put one through
Mrs Vaughan's door.

Mrs Vaughan lived round the corner in Heather Close and had a reputation for :kidnapping: pets and pretending she thought they were stray. She had kidnapped Cat several times and Fatty once, even though she knew they were our pets and Fatty was on a lead.

Then she would phone the RSPCA and say she'd found a stray.

Myf said, 'Well, at least she's an animal l♥ver. We can't be choosy about our customers.'

'But what if she kidnaps the zoo?' Roobs said worriedly.

That's when I spotted Cat at Mrs Vaughan's window mouthing 'miaow'.

'That's our cat!' I said and rang on the door bell. It took Mrs Vaughan ages to get to the door. She is a <u>HOARDER</u>, Mum says, which means her house is full of useless JUNK and she never throws anything away.

When she finally opened the door, Cat came running out but then started miaowing to go back in, which is how I knew she was our cat. Since we got Fatty, Cat found it hard to settle (Fatty was always either eating her food or chasing her up the garden) and when she was inside she wanted to go out . . .

. . . and when she was outside she wanted to come in.

Meanwhile, Myf had handed Mrs V a leaflet.

'I hope there won't be any endangered species at this zoo? And that all the conditions are legal?' Mrs Vaughan called after us, pointing to the picture of the elephant on the leaflet.

'See!' Myf cried, proudly pointing at her drawing. '<u>She</u> recognises it as an elephant!'

Cat went happily back into Mrs Vaughan's without a backward glance, which was actually **quite** hurtful.

'OK, Cat!' I called to her, trying for a casual tone. 'You can stay for a while, but we want you back by dusk!'

(Straight away, she started miaowing at the window to come out again. Mrs Vaughan would be bound to get fed up with her before she rang the RSCPA.)

We had one more leaflet to deliver, to Roger Lovely's house.

He was his usual <u>wonderful</u> self when he opened the door.

Thank you, Jells. My little sister Dilly is very excited about the zoo.

'See you soon,' he said and closed the door.

It was my idea!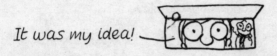

I reminded him.

-6-
Low Fatty Diet

Mum's mum, my gran, has got wind of the wedding and has started coming over to 'help'. Which basically means making herself comfy, criticising everyone and wondering what sort of hat she should wear.

My gran isn't a nice, cuddly, friendly gran, she is a **bony**, selfish gran who tried to make us call her **Carol** (her name). But we actually call her **Grarol** because when we were little we would go to call her Gran, 'Gra—' and she would dart us an evil **look** (especially if there were good-looking men her own age around) . . .

Good-looking man

Gra . . .

. . . rol?

. . . and we would change it mid-word to **Grarol**. She didn't like being called Grarol but it was a good compromise and better than Gran, she thought.

Grarol says things that are so *subtly* mean, that you don't realise she's been mean until later, and even then you're not sure if she's been deliberately mean or just innocently tactless.

Like when Jay got a place at the Boxford Football Academy:

Oh, were they short of candidates this year then?

**OR**

You've been comfort eating again, haven't you, darling? It suits you being fatter in the face.

OR

That weight loss is very
ageing, Susan.

 OR

Aah, she looks like a little baby
elephant with her sticky-outy ears!

(I was still called
Roberta then)

As soon as she saw me eating a slice of
toast, she said,

'Jelly! Have you <u>any</u> idea how many
calories are in a piece of buttered
toast?!'

I told her I had <u>no</u> idea and couldn't
care less and went back to debating with

Roobs whether or not to have another bit, or TWO other bits.

While we waited for our THREE bits of toast each, I could hear her saying to Mum,

'A dress like that at your age, darling? Well if it's what you want . . . _terribly_ unflattering on someone flat-chested, mind.'

Then she turned her attention to Fatty who was doing lazy begging under the toaster.

'Oh my! The size of that dog! It's cruel to let him get like that!' Grarol exclaimed.

'He was born like that,' Mum said, defensively.

'He's got big bones,' I added.

'And a slow metabolism,' Jay interjected. It was a rare moment of family harmony.

Rubbish! He'll have to go on a diet!

And I think everyone could do with eating more sensibly, it'll help Fatty.

Mum was just about to protest when Grarol said,

'I'm just thinking of you, darling. Don't you want everyone to look their best on the **BIG** day?' and she put her hand on Mum's shoulder.

c°nfᵘᶻᵉd by this rare show of affection Mum stuttered, 'Well, er, I suppose so . . .'

So Grarol put Fatty on a diet starting **right there and then**. She said she would stay and do dinner for everyone. She made roast chicken and salad.

That's yours Fatty, make sure
you chew each mouthful 30 times.

We all had:

1 slice of cucumber, 1 small piece of chicken

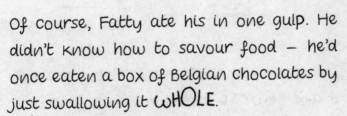

Of course, Fatty ate his in one gulp. He
didn't know how to savour food — he'd
once eaten a box of Belgian chocolates by
just swallowing it WHOLE.

I'll take the plates out.

How helpful, Jelly.

Jelly! Put that bird down!

I dropped the chicken and Fatty grabbed it and :burst: through the cat flap . . .

. . . and sat scoffing the chicken in the garden with the cat flap round his 'waist'.

Is That a Rumble I Can Hear?

Disaster! Billy Rumble has been moved into our maths class! Mr Fairman our head teacher has decided to move **disruptive** kids into relatively well-behaved classes in the hope that it will have a calming effect on them. Of course it's had the opposite effect and all the relatively well-behaved kids have become disruptive

Billy's one of those people who is really good at **spotting** people's physical faults just when they were feeling relieved no one

had noticed. Billy picks up on the slightly crooked nose, the knocked knees, the spotty forehead and the wobbly bottom, thinks up a name and then begins his torture.

Well, on day two I saw him scrutinising me and he noticed/decided that I have big ears and has started calling me 'Dumbo'. It is a <u>long</u> time since anyone has mentioned my ears — in fact, I think the last person was Grarol when I was 6, and it took me years to get over it. Insults just stay with you, sometimes for life. My heart sank when he caught my eye and said,

Alright, Dumbo?

Half the class have heard of the Disney classic so think it's because I have big ears,

the other half just assume I am **THICK**.

Anyway, they all **LAUGHED** along nervously with Billy.

I am trying to keep my head (and ears) down and am very TENSE – sometimes he forgets but then out of the blue he will casually glance my way and go,

Dumbo-o-o

Ha, ha, ha, ha, ha

and everyone roars with laughter. Well, except Myf and Roobs. Roobs because she isn't there, she's in the genius maths group, and Myf cos she's FIERCELY loyal –

Look, Billy, there's nothing wrong with having ginormous sticky-outy ears like an elephant, so shuddup!

. . . but not a lot of help.

I spent the next few nights examining my ears and fantasising about having an operation to have them pinned back.

-8-
Rule Brittainee

Now something **REALLY** terrible has happened! Worse than Billy being moved into our class. My mum's friend's daughter Brittainee from L.A. has moved into my bedroom!!!

She is staying with us for a WHOLE month before the wedding because she wants to 'do' Europe and Mum has put her in **MY** bedroom with **ME**!

She has been in (my) bed all day because she has '**jet lag**' (sounds disgusting!). I can't even go in there in the day because she screams at me to . . . *GED OUT!!*

(She has become *nocturnal* and sleeps all day and is up all night.)

When I was finally allowed in at 10 p.m. and got into my bed (cushions on floor) she was up making Skype calls to America and saying everything about Europe (by which she meant Boxford, England) **sucked**...

The food, → the weather, → the accent, → the TV, → the houses, → the cars, → the beds...

...I nearly lost it at that point as I find my bed **VERY** comfortable and *she* was in it!

When she finally went to have a shower, I crawled into my own bed. Then she came and sat on me and when I screamed she started screaming.

Aaah! There's a strange man in 'my' bed!

Mum made me take her out to show her Boxford but all she wanted to do was go to McDonald's where she went ~~on and on~~ about Jay and how everything about Europe **sucked** except Jay as he was really 'h☀t.'

(She is obviously mad, or 'CRAZY' as she would say.)

Brittainee's ~~mum~~ mom is my ~~mom~~ mum's friend from school who went to live in America. When I complained about Brittainee, mum got cross and said I had

to look after her as she didn't want her
~~mu~~ mom thinking Brittainee wasn't having
a good time, as she was always saying
how the US was SO much better and
how . . .

England **SUCKS**.

(Like mother like daughter.)

-9-
The Price of Beauty

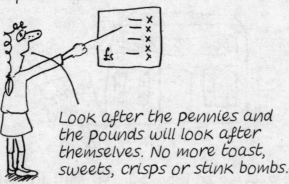

At the next Faithful Club meeting Roobs elected herself treasurer and said we must scrimp and save.

Look after the pennies and the pounds will look after themselves. No more toast, sweets, crisps or stink bombs.

OK, toast is allowed . . .

she said, as our panic-stricken eyes met.

She said there was no point just waiting for the zoo, we should utilise (**posh** word for 'use') our time on another business idea. After a lot of debating (stupid ideas) we decided to open a **beauty** parlour in the shed using home-made products. Mum says even in a recession people still want to look nice.

We decided to have our GRAND OPENING the next day because Mum and Julian were taking Brittainee to see the sights (which she said would all **suck**, except M+M World). We undercut all the local beauty parlours by a LOT for treatments but were selling our home-made beauty products at the counter at extortionate price$.

Cashmere and Silk Rose
Vanilla Shine Smooth Elixir
Shampoo
(**secret ingredients**: washing-up
liquid, potpourri, bobbles from bobbly
2% cashmere jumper)

Mirror Shine Platinum
Super Smooth Lustre Spray
(**secret ingredients**: Mr Sheen, Glue)

Olive and Spice
Drench Moisture Masque
(**secret ingredients**: olive oil,
medium curry powder)

60 Second Tough Candy High
Shine Nail Varnish
(**secret ingredients**: Julian's car paint
from cellar)

Grarol, being stingy **AND** vain, was our first customer. After commenting on Fatty's weight gain,

I SEE THE DIET ISN'T WORKING!

in a **VERY** LOUD voice, she then began to whisper,

'Pensioner's deal, please — The Faithful Beauty Package.'

You mean for the well-over-65s?

Myf yelled.

(Thinks Grarol is DEAF.)

The deal included: Eyebrow tidy, Wash 'n' blow dry, Facial, Manicure.

It was Myf's job to do the eyebrow tidy.

Hold **still**, Grarol.

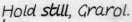

Ow!

She took **AGES**! (Roobs, Fatty and I took the opportunity to go and eat some toast while Grarol was incapacitated.)

She didn't stand back to assess her handiwork, she just kept tidying.

Just this one, this one, hold on,
just tidy this one . . .

When she finally **did** stand back, Grarol's eyebrows looked **very** tidy — i.e. she didn't have any.

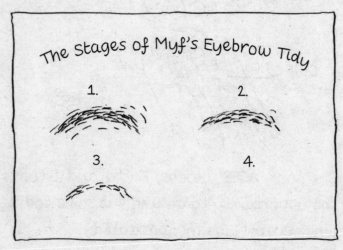

The Stages of Myf's Eyebrow Tidy

1.

2.

3.

4.

It was like when Julian cut the privet hedge.

JULIAN!

Ooer . . .

What?

S'alright, Grarol, I'm just going to apply some tint.

Just as Myf was **tattooing** Grarol's eyebrows back on → Fatty leapt towards our hand-made **beauty** products, detecting something possibly edible.

FATTY!

The marker pen slipped and made Grarol look permanently PERPLEXED →

We managed to keep Grarol away from a mirror until Roobs had shampooed her hair and I had done the manicure and facial.

I can smell toast.

There was so much ⋅foAm⋅ from the shampoo (washing-up liquid) that Myf had to hose Grarol down in the garden.

We ~~blew-dry~~ ~~blew-dried~~ ~~bloo-drood~~ blow-dried her hair so it covered her eyebrows and took the lenses out of her glasses.

Lovely! It takes years off me! I look half my age.

Blurry image

Would you like me to do your moustache, modom?

I BEG your PARDON?

Many mature ladies look very attractive with a moustache, I have noticed, it's quite the fashion with the over-80's. A Faithful Tattooed Moustache will last up to 3 years.

good-looking man

That sounds maist interesting,
I maight bring mai grandmother
in for one . . . tee-hee!

She paid her £20 fee (which was a bargain
for seven hours' work) and purchased
some Cashmere and Silk Rose Vanilla Shine
Smooth Elixir shampoo for £7 and scurried
off.

We made £27.00 from the beauty parlour
Total: £27.00 in our kitty for O.M.G.!

–10–
False Advertising

(*No animals were harmed in the writing of the next two chapters.)

The day of the zoo arrived. Myf and Roobs were so $_E{}^{XC'}T_E{}^D$ they turned up at my house at 6 a.m., which was fine by me as I was already awake listening to the sound of Brittainee yacking on Skype; her bed time wasn't for several hours.

Myf set about drawing a huge poster which she attached to the privet hedge out the front . . .

TODAY!

ZOO

(It was my idea Roger. Myf x)

ENTRANCE: £2

Refreshments!

2.00 P.M.

BE THERE OR BE ZOOPID!

. . . while Roobs and I made sandwiches. Roob's uncle runs a sandwich shop in the city and he told her that the trick is to put the filling in the centre of the bread

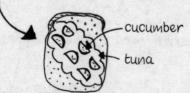

cucumber

tuna

so when you slice it
it looks really *full* but actually isn't

This strikes me as a bit stingy but Roobs says if we want to get tickets for O.M.G.! we have to be ruthless business women.

At 1 o'clock we thought we'd better gather the animals together and line them up along the garden path. First of all we got Fatty and tied him to a tree. He's not TOTALLY THICK because he did realise he was probably **not** going for a walk and started singing very LOUDLY (and soul-fully I felt).

What a racket!

ROWOOOOOH!

Shuddup, Myf, he's got a lovely voice.

(Only I am allowed to insult Fatty, remember.)

Then we found Cat miaowing at the window to come outside. Myf picked her up (all WRONG) and placed her at the top of the path. But she ran to the door and started miaowing to go in, so we decided to hang her FAVOURITE cat-nip-filled mouse from a branch just above her and she started dancing about wildly,

trying to swipe it

'She's dancing!' cried Myf.

The sight of Cat DISCO dancing just out of the reach of his teeth made Fatty sing even louder

I felt guilty about using Fatty and Cat as exhibits for commercial gain. But Myf and Roobs don't understand . . .

PET

GUILT

Myf, ever the thicko, said,

'They love it!'

And Roobs, ever the hard-nosed business woman, wrote:

 and

on to green and pink luminous STARS from her uncle's sandwich shop and stuck them on the poster out the front.

Then we got Fishcake out, but his tank was a bit green and slimy. I tried to clean it with a toothbrush but every time I cleaned a bit, Fishcake hid behind another bit until he was in his castle and wouldn't come out

'I know!' screeched Myf, bordering on hysteria.

'Invisible Fish!!'

And she wrote it on a luminous star and stuck it on the poster outside.

Then we got the guinea pigs, Guinness and Blossom, in their run. Julian's prize curly kale was tantalisingly out of reach in the vegetable patch and they started squealing like actual pigs . . .

Myf wrote 'Real Life Miniature Furry Pigs' on a luminous star and added it to the poster

Then we put the hamster's cage on the path. The howling, dancing and squealing made Hamwich very anxious and when Hamwich gets anxious he gets in his wheel and goes round so fast you can't see his wheel or his legs and he just looks like an orange blur FLOATING in his cage.

Even Roobs recognised that Myf had gone mad now, and she sobered up.

Last, we put the mice on the path. Pearl and Dean were always either asleep or trying to escape. (They had succeeded **many** times but could always be lured back **eventually** with peanut butter sandwiches

. . . even with stingy filling.)

Anyway, today they were asleep in their nest.

We can't have more invisible animals!!

Myf cried, and opened the cage and poked the nest with the toothbrush, at which point Pearl and Dean le**a**pt out from behind the water bottle where they had been hiding and ran into the garden.

(I could have sworn they had deliberately put two monkey nuts in their nest to look like them sleeping . . .

. . . but their brains are only this big

z z z z   Z z z z

. . . So maybe not!?)

We could see them peeping round flowers, rocks and old tyres but couldn't catch them.

'I know!' I cried. 'The peanut butter sandwiches! We can lure them back!'

70

'Ere, Jelly, you got any more of those peanut butter sandwiches? I don't like them tuna cat food ones.

RICKY!!

He'd eaten ALL the peanut butter sand-wiches! But Roobs had an idea . . .

I know!

wild mice!

Real live mice – like a safari!

Myf was, by now, **totally** deranged.

Ha, ha, ha, ha, ha!

ROWOO!

It's NOT FUNNY, Myf.

squoink!

Squoink!

. . . and I felt **VERY** guilty . . . until my bedroom window *juddered* open and Brittainee appeared.

Can you pa-lease keep the noise down! I'm tryin' to sleep!!!

Then I felt guilty that I was using my pets to make money but pleased they were annoying Brittainee.

TODAY!

ZOO

(It was my idea Roger. MYF x)

WILD MICE SAFARI!

SENSATIONAL SINGING DOG!

INVISIBLE FISH!

ENTRANCE: £2

Refreshments!

2.00 P.M.

DISCO DANCING CAT!

FANTASTIC FLYING HAMSTER!

BE THERE OR BE ZOOPID!

REAL LIFE MINIATURE FURRY PIGS!

–11–
Exotic Animals

Finally, all the animals were arranged and it was 1.55 p.m. so we sat down and waited for paying customers.

1.59 Myf said, 'One minute to go.'

2 p.m. No one arrived.

2.11 Ricky burped.

2.29 No one came.

2.37 Roobs went to the loo.

2.41 Roobs came back from the loo.

3 p.m. We ate the tuna sandwiches (Roobs made us pay) and drank the over-diluted Ribena.

By **3.30** the animals were all asleep. Even the mice were back in their nest.

Then at **3.36** there was a scraping noise from the back gate.

It was Bethany Iceland with the cool girls. They barged in refusing to pay the £2 entry.

Got any Diet Coke?

What is this, Befny?

All the animals are **dead**.

They're just tired — you still have to pay.

Shu' up My *FANNY!*

not bothered.

THEN the worst thing that could possibly happen happened — Billy Rumble came stalking in.

'Ere, Billy, all the animals are dead!

Bethany complained.

Billy looked around, then stared at me for slightly too long. I looked at my feet to avoid his gaze ⊙ ⊙. My ears were throbbing and felt GINORMOUS.

The air crackled.

Usually if you try and guess what's about to happen, it doesn't happen. But what I'd guessed was about to happen **DID** happen.

There is one animal I can see that's still alive . . . !

Bethany and the CGs started laughing hysterically o o o o o o o

Dumbo!

That's hilarious!

Amid all this of course Roger arrived with his sister Dilly who was squealing with excitement,

I've never sawn a zoo before!!

My bedroom window trundled open again, and Brittainee squawked,

For Chrissakes!! What the heck is going on??

(gruff voice)

Oh, hi, Rog, how are you?

(gooey giggly voice)

All the noise woke Fatty up, and the first things he saw were Bethany's quivering buttocks.

He can't stand hysterical teenage girls but he loves quivering bottoms — they remind him of the jelly in his dog food — so he decided to bite them.

Bethany made a **ginormous fuss**. It didn't even hurt! (As Jay always says to me after he's thumped me one.)

But I attended to her anyway because I didn't want her to sue Fatty, and I was pleased that her bum (W) was distracting Billy from my ears. ?)

Dilly was approaching the animals still squealing with excitement and woke all the rest of them from their naps and they resumed their previous antics.

She giggled helplessly at Cat dancing, and tried to stroke her fur the **WRONG** way. ⟶

Then she moved on to Fishcake.

'There's nothing in there!' she wailed.

'Invisible fish!' I called. 'Didn't you read the poster?!'

Ooh, Woger! Invisisabubble fish! I've never sawn any of those before!

she cried, jumping up and down with excitement.

'Oh look, Woger! That dog is singing a song!' And she ran towards Fatty, who was *straining* at the lead and whose singing had started to sound like ((growling)).

It was then that I remembered that it wasn't just hysterical teenage girls that Fatty hated: he hated hysterical children under 3 feet tall even more. Fatty was about to bite Dilly . . .

My life FLASHED before me and I had just got to the bit where I was in prison for keeping a dangerous dog and Myf and Roobs were visiting and smuggling in a fruit cake with a file hidden in it  when Fatty ═disappeared into thin :air:, millimetres from biting Dilly's nose off . . .

waaah!

Mrs Vaughan had captured him with a large fishing net — poor starved unwanted stray that he was.

(I loved Mrs Vaughan ♡ very deeply at that moment.)

Jelly 4 Mrs V

–12–
Count Fatcula

Even though Fatty's fangs hadn't made contact with her nose, Dilly was still screaming her head off ↘

waaah!

Roger was saying,

'I'd better take her home, she's suffering from shock.'

Bethany fluttered her eyelashes ～～ ～～ ～～ ～～ ～～ (to which she'd had time to reapply mascara despite being in 'agony').

What about me, Roger? I'm suffering from shock too, you know,

she said in a voice even more babyish than Dilly's.

So Roger took Bethany and the cool girls home for hot **sweet** tea.

'Oi, Befny, where you going?' Billy demanded.

'Shuddup, loser!' Bethany told him.

Billy was in a right royal **BAD** mood now, so he called me 'Dumbo' one more time before taking the last of the sandwiches and stomping off.

'Oi! You didn't pay!' Myf shouted.

'At least Roger didn't take back his £2,' Roobs said, writing it in our accounts book.

We had just sighed with relief that it was all over when Jay and his idiot mates, Jock and Brendan from Year 11, turned up . . .

Go away, Jay.

Stop showing off, Jelly. ←
(Jay's catchphrase)

Jay said, 'I hear the **FAT** one has disgraced himself again — L🙂ckily, Roger's sister is fine. Anyway where IS Fatty? Mum says his pageboy outfit has arrived from eBay.'

Hurr, hurr, dog in clothes, stupid.

Jock and Brendan sniggered.

I felt quite defensive about Mum and Fatty.

'If my mum wants to have Fatty as her pageboy, she is entitled,' I told them.

Brendan and Jock went PINK (They seem to find me more alarming now I am more mature.)

Then, oh **JOY**, Karen and Cheryl (Kaz and Chez — my cross-country 'running' partners) were cᴌᴀ̓ᴛ̓ᴇ̓ᴿ̓ɪ̓ɴɢ up the side alley.

'Oh-oh, this'll be good,' Jay said to Jock and Brendan. 'Let's stick around.'

Jock and Brendan said 'Hurr, hurr'.

Alright Jez? Alright Jayz, Alright Brendz?
Alright Jockz? Alright Myfz? Alright Roobz?

They paid the entrance fee and Kaz said,

So where's this elephant then?
Billy said there was an elephant.

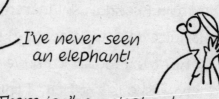

I've never seen
an elephant!

There isn't an elephant.

Wha'?

It's a con!

I'm the elephant.

Wha'?

There was no point trying to explain, so I
tried to distract them.

'We have lots of other exotic animals—'
I started to tell them, but suddenly Chez
was screaming.

'What is it now, Chez?' Kaz said irritably.

'Rats!' Chez said.

'They're not rats, they're guinea pigs,' I
told them.

A rat!

A rat!

It's not a rat, it's a mouse.

Then they stood in front of each animal
and screamed.

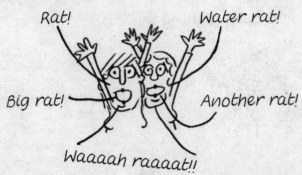

Rat!

Water rat!

Big rat!

Another rat!

Waaaah raaaat!!

Then Jay re-appeared with his locust
tank........

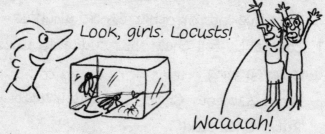

Look, *girls.* Locusts!

Waaaah!

Kaz and Chez ran fast enough to win a
cross-country race without cheating,
dropping small change  as they went.

Jock and Brendan looked like they were
going to wet themselves
laughing, and Myf and
Roobs were joining in.

Tee, hee...

'It's not **<u>FUNNY</u>**,' I told them.

'How much have we got?' Myf asked, later.

Um, let me see, Roobs replied. 10, 20, 30 . . . . £6.30.

'Useless!' Myf cried. 'We're going to have to think of more ways to earn money.'

Then, when I went to take the poster down from the privet hedge, I saw Billy had vandalised it . . . .

"DUMBO"

Daughter of JUMBO.

. . . and abandoned a sandwich that he hadn't paid for. I was just putting the sandwich in my mouth when Myf cried,

'*LOOK* Jelly! Look who it is!'

'Oh what _NOW_?!', I snapped, ~~cat food~~ tuna falling down my front.

'It's Sandy Blatch! The one you fancied

cos he looked like Buster Bauble from O.M.G.! she yelled.

'Oh gawd,' I muttered and pushed myself into the privet hedge behind the poster.

'But he was too short,' Myf continued loudly. 'But then he grew tall . . .'

Meanwhile, Sandy was trooping past and was going . . . up my garden path! He was carrying a keyboard and was followed by two other boys and Benji Butler with an electric guitar. Fortunately, they all had their headphones on.

Benji Butler stopped and looked with interest at the poster as Myf finished her shouting . . .

'BUt then he started going out with Angel Farraday!'

'Shut up, Myf,' I muttered from behind the poster.

Jelly? Is that you?

. . . Benji replied, looking at the picture of me as an elephant.

'Excuse me . . . whatever your name is,' Myf demanded of Benji,

Why are you going in Jelly's house?

Oh hello, Myfanwy! Well, you see, Jelly's mama has booked our band So.M.G.! to play at her wedding. We're an O.M.G.! tribute band. Some people seem to think that our lead singer and keyboardist looks like Buster Bauble!

I blushed crimson inside the hedge.

'We've got an opening for a tambourine player if ever you were interested,' Benji told Myf, and walked off whistling the O.M.G.! hit . . .   SH-ORT GIRL

'Oh no!' I said, still disguised as a privet hedge. 'They're playing at Mum's wedding!'

That's the last straw!

Roobs said,

I think Benji Butler has a crush on you, Myf.

Who's Benji Butler?

↑
Short **AND** dim girl.

-13-
So.M.G.!

As soon as So.M.G.! had left I stormed into the house.

 I can't believe you've asked Sandy Blatch's tribute band to play at your wedding!!

Mum dragged her eyes away from the tiara she was trying on Cat.

I thought you liked Sandy Blatch — last time I heard.

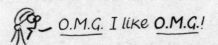

And I thought you liked So.M.G.! Honestly, I can't win!

 O.M.G. I like **O.M.G.**!

'Who's Sandy Blatch?' Brittainee asked, entering the room and **draping** herself

91

on the sofa. She was over her jet lag apparently but too tired to do anything except be waited on.

'Is he hot?'

'Well,' Myf began, 'Jelly thinks he looks like Buster Bauble from O.M.G.!'

'Shut up, Myf,' I said. I didn't want Brittainee getting her fangs into Sandy. Mum had said she was a 'man-eater' like her mother, Jane, and at that moment, braces *glinting*, she did have something of the cannibal about her.

'He's got a girlfriend,' said Roobs.

'*Has* he?' Mum said, seemingly **surprised** that she wasn't privy to information reserved for the under-14s market and that really shouldn't be interesting to anyone over 40.

'Angel Farraday!' Myf pronounced **LOUDLY**.

'Oh, well', Mum said. 'He was asking

after you, Jells, so I thought he was still sweet on you.'

Really??

Anyway, I'm not interested. He's got a girlfriend and I'm not interested anyway,

I added.

 I AM!

If he looks like Buster Bauble! When can I meet him?

I thought you had a crush on Jay!

Roobs said, as Jay came in the room.

I have, but a girl has to keep her options open . . . Ooh, sorry, Jayby! You're still my number one!

Jay went scarlet.

 I don't care, do what you like, where're my football boots, Mum?

And he scurried out of the room before she could answer.

 Mwah!

'Mum, you'll have to get another band,' I insisted.

'No, Jelly,' Mum began, 'they are very . . .'

 *Cheap!*

Julian interjected.

'Free, in fact,' Mum said proudly. 'They just want the practice, apparently . . .' Mum winked at me. 'Or maybe Sandy wants an **EXCUSE** to see you in the summer holidays?'

'Shut up, Mum.' I told her.

(When in doubt, say shut up.)

-14-

Unobtainabubble

Hurraaay! It's the summer holidays! Only problem is, Mum has said it's OK for Sandy and So.M.G.! to practise in our garage when they need to. I am :LIVID: – they have already been here _twice_ and I've literally had to _hide_ until they've gone.

So far I had managed to disguise myself as:

a) A privet hedge

 b) A curtain

c) A rug

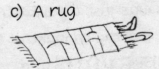

I say **had** to hide, I didn't **have** to, no one made me, but I just did hide and I don't know why.

I was feeling c°nfᵤᵻᵉd. I really didn't have time for thoughts of actual boys. I had my work cut out thinking of ways to raise money for our O.M.G.! tickets.

It was easy to have a crush on Roger Lovely— all I had to do was **blush** occasionally, stare at the side of his face and kiss my grandmother's bust of Napoleon pretending it was him.

It was just a bit of **FUN**. I didn't **really** fancy him. He was a bit thick — and I knew he would never go out with me — so it was just a fantasy.

But the thought of Sandy made me very **NERVOUS** and now I felt properly anxious about the wedding.

I asked Julian about it and he said that **Röger Lövely** was something called 'unobtainable' so it was SAFE to have a crush on him — a bit like having a crush on Buster Bauble.

He was as likely to step out of the poster and ask me to go to the cinema with him . . .

oo - er!

Hi!

. . . as **Röger** was to see me as a potential girlfriend.

Whereas Sandy was (or had been) obtainable and had then

become unobtainable ——→
which was the worst kind,
apparently. Julian said I was NERVOUS
because a **bit** of me wanted to obtain him,
and I knew, because he *had* had a crush on
me before, that this might not
be a **complete** impossibility.

I didn't really feel any wiser but I still
felt NERVOUS at the thought of seeing him.

When Cousin Amelia came round for a
street-dance rehearsal I insisted we go to
the park so we wouldn't bump into Sandy
in the garden. Myf was being **VERY** bossy.

> Right, all get in a line and
> just follow my moves.
> A-one, a-two,
> a-one, two, three, four!

Then she just stood with her back
to us and started throwing herself about.
She was just like Melanie the teacher; she

expected us to follow her and had no idea what we were doing. Amelia did a sort of balletic version, and Brittainee, Roobs and I moved around like a six-legged beast — vaguely in the right direction — jumping, frolicking and tripping over each other.

When Myf leapt to her final position, she turned to face us.

How did it go?

It sucked but I was great.

Fine.

Piece of cake.

Where?

'Great!' said Myf. 'I think we're ready, guys!'

-15-
Junk and Disorderly

Myf, Roobs, Ricky and I were in the shed counting up our money from the zoo and the b𝓮𝓪uty salon. We only had £33.30 and we needed £200. We were feeling a bit desperate when Jay came barging in.

'Mum says don't forget the wedding meeting and bridesmaids' fitting tonight and where's Fatty?'

Oh gawd! I'd forgotten all about Fatty! He was still at Mrs Vaughan's! He'd been there for days and no one had noticed! I had wondered why Cat seemed so relaxed.

Myf, Roobs, Ricky and I stomped round to Mrs Vaughan's and looked through the window . . . through all the junk, books and plants I could just about make out Fatty scoffing from a bowl. Then he lay down, looking very **FAT**, and a hand entered the picture and tickled his tummy. I banged on the door and saw Mrs Vaughan and Fatty hide behind the door frame. So I did some plaintive *miaowing* – the kind a starving, stray cat might do – and Mrs V came to the door.

'Oh, hello,' she said. 'I thought I heard a starving stray cat.'

'Is our dog Fatty here?'

'Um, I don't think . . .'

Then Ricky rustled a crisp packet and of course Fatty came straight away.

'This is Neville,' Mrs Vaughan said.

'He's not called Neville, Mrs Vaughan, he's called Fatty,' Myf informed her.

'Oh,' Mrs Vaughan said quietly. 'I call him Neville.'

'I'm sorry, Mrs Vaughan, but . . . Neville has to go home now,' I told her.

'Mrs Vaughan?' Myf said. 'If you like dogs and cats so much, why don't you get your own instead of stealing other people's?'

'Myf,' Roobs whispered. 'Don't be so rude.'

'I don't steal them, I just rescue them for a bit.'

'But why don't you get your own?'

'Well,' Mrs Vaughan said, 'it's a long story.'

Mrs Vaughan invited us in for tea, which was quite difficult as the house was so crammed full of stuff there was only a tiny space in the kitchen and we all had to stand up to drink from our mugs. Mrs V told us she used to run a pet boarding house with her husband, but when her husband died she couldn't really cope with the house and the animals. She stopped throwing stuff away, like newspapers and bottles, and started collecting stuff like books and junk. When her house was full she started filling up the garden too, which meant she couldn't look after the dogs and cats properly and owners stopped bringing their pets.

Ever since then she hasn't had the energy to sort the house out, but still liked animals so started rescuing strays (we didn't like to correct her).

Nice comfy bed

Then we all stood around clearing our throats. No one could think of anything to say, so we all looked at Neville/Fatty and made the occasional comment.

'He's looking at that fly.'
'Ooh, look he's
got an itch.'
Etc., etc.

'Ahem,' I said. 'Mrs Vaughan, we have to take Neville back now.'

'OK', Mrs Vaughan said, sniffing. 'Bye bye, Neville.' She had tears in her eyes as she waved us off.

'I feel sorry for Mrs Vaughan,' Myf said. 'Maybe we should help her clear her house?' Ricky suggested. 'Then she could open her pet hotel again?'

So Myf, Roobs, Ricky and I spent all day helping clear Mrs V's house. She found it very <u>hard</u> to watch her stuff going into bags so after she explained how to put it in three different piles in the front garden:

we suggested she take 'Neville' out for a

very long walk

When Mrs V got back we had cleared the **WHOLE** house and garden. Underneath all the stuff was a really nice comfy house and in the garden all the old accommodation for the dogs and cats. It looked so appealing that Fatty got straight into one of the kennels and went to sleep.

We'd even unearthed the sign:

VAUGHAN'S PETOTEL

Mrs V burst into tears and said how would she ever thank us. She said why didn't we all take something from one of the piles.

I took a Banana Guard, Myf took a glass vase shaped like a fish, Roobs chose a Filofax and Ricky chose a newspaper dating from the day he was born.

-16-
Jelly Mould

When we got back, So.M.G.! were practising in the garage. Myf and Roobs virtually galloped past the garage doors they were so excited about the bridesmaids' fitting, but I sidled past, tucking my ears in my hair beforehand.

Even though I told myself not to *LOOK*, I couldn't resist a little glance in, and there was Sandy right in front of me.

Hi, Jelly!

Hello,

I said in a voice that came out like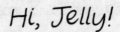

'Fancy coming in to watch us rehearse? We're just doing another 20 minutes . . .'

I shook my head and my ears slipped out. I tried to tuck them in my hair again.

'Don't!' Sandy said. 'You shouldn't take any notice of Billy — you've got really cute ears.'

I felt my face **burning** but I couldn't risk pulling my curtain hair across without making my ears pop out again and I became aware of him staring at my Banana Guard. So I stupidly turned my back on him.

-Godda go — bridesmaids' fitting. Bye!

Then I did funny skating-style walking away so my ears wouldn't pop out and ran into the house with my cheeks **burning**.

'You're as *red* as a tomato, Jelly,'
Grarol remarked.

'I've just run from the garage.'

'You really should get more exercise.'
she told me.

First on the agenda was Jay's speech.

Have you written
your speech?

Chill, Mum. I'll
just improvise.

Well, I think you
should learn it — you
might get nervous.

Nervous? I'm totally relaxed
about it. I'll just be myself.

That's what I'm
worried about . . .

And what about the stag do?

I don't want a stag do, Sue –
I don't know anyone . . .

Don't be silly, Julian – there's Dot's
husband Alan and, er, Jay . . .

Don't worry, Mum, it's
all under control.

Right . . . bridesmaids' street-
dance routine? How's it going?

It sucks.

Well, obviously I've got a
dance background and
I'm quite good but . . .

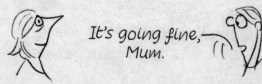
It's going fine,
Mum.

I found that whereas before I imagined everything at the wedding through Roger's eyes, now I saw everything through Sandy's eyes →

Urgh! I felt SICK!

I'm choreographing it, Mrs Rowntree.

Mrs Rowntree for NOW, Myf, soon to be Mrs Mould.

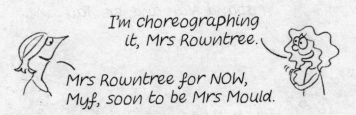

Hee, hee, hee! ___   ___ That sucks!

 ─ What's so funny?

It's a bit of a gross name . . .

It is a bit rubbish, Mum.

Yeah, Mum.

Well, you'd better get used
to it because you two are
taking it too.

 No way!

We're not changing our
names again, I like Rowntree.

 They really don't have to, Susan.

 Will you be quiet, Julian!

Anyway, hard luck, you're
changing it. This marriage
is my last so you'd better
get used to it.

 It might not be
Susan, I mean,
you never know,
we might—

SHUT UP, JULIAN!

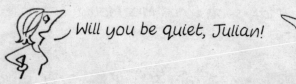

That means I'll be . . .

Jelly Mould!

Haa-aa-aahahahah!

(collecting herself)

Why's that funny?

Cos it's what you make a jelly in!

And it means you're all mouldy!

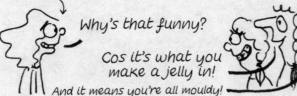

Gross!

(Finally getting the joke)

Ha, ha, ha, ha . . .

-17-
Blooming Bridesmaids

Then it was time for the bridesmaids' fittings so we all trooped upstairs.

Dot got the dresses out of a large bag. They were completely over the top.

Puffy → and ← frilly

like giant PINK! meringues.

Of course, Myf and Roobs were beside themselves. I was beside myself as well . . . with horror. But I did see one positive thing about them.

'Mum, we can't possibly do street dance in these.'

'Ah! We thought of that, didn't we, Dot?

Dot has made special matching pants to wear underneath to preserve your modesty.'

'So when you do backflips etc. your nether regions will be covered.'

Poor deluded mother. The only nether regions that needed covering were Myf's and those pants were way too **BIG**.

Then Mum put Cat in her outfit and Dot tried to get Fatty's ring-bearing sash round his increased middle without Grarol seeing.

Then it was the big moment: Mum trying on her meringue. She **squEEzed** it on.

Ooh – it's a bit tight.

I can still get into my wedding dress from when I was 21!

Yeah, well bully for you. And can you take that look off your face?

What look?

'I think you look gorgeous, Sue,' said Dot.

'Thank you, Dot. Anyway, everyone, Brittainee's kindly agreed to do hair and make-up on the wedding morning,' Mum explained.

'You limeys really need some grooming!'

'I've just been groomed!' Grarol said with her permanently perplexed expression.

You need new face furniture, 'Grandma'! Those glasses suck!

I beg your pardon?

Mum couldn't help tittering . . .

. . . until Brittainee and Amelia put their dresses on and looked quite put out.

116

Sue, this dress sucks!

To be honest, Auntie Sue, I don't really suit pink.

Well, I'm SO sorry. Would you like me to get Kate Middleton's designer in?

She sucks. Wod aboud Victoria Beckham?

Well, that would be preferable.

I could see Mum was going to blow . . . Through ~~gritted~~ teeth, she said,

'Jelly! Why don't you take Amelia and Brittainee to your shed for a bridesmaids' get-together? You can show them your guinea pigs.'

'For a fee,' I muttered.

'Yes, I think 40p each and an extra 10p per stroke is fair,' Roobs said, taking me seriously.

117

-18-
Bums in the Pool

I showed Guinness and Blossom to Brittainee and she said they **sucked** – pigs in the US were **ENORMOUS** and bald.

No wonder you limeys are all so skinny!

I _slightly_ liked her for a nanosecond for saying we were skinny but then she started talking about the hen night.

So what's the deal with the bachelorette party?

She means hen party.

It's all perfectly under control, thank you. We're having a pool party . . .

You godda pool!?!

. . . at the local baths.

 Urgh! Bums* use those to wash!

ANYWAY . . . then a Happy Meal and then back here for film, popcorn and sleepover.

Ha ha ha! That todally sucks!

Hee hee.

A-heee!

Hee?

Chuckle.

Except Brittainee, these people have no idea why they're laughing.

 What we're gonna do is limo picks us up, chocolate making, pole dancing, weekend in Paris-France, spa, caberet, wine tasting . . .

* American for 'tramp'

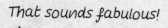

That sounds fabulous!

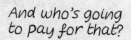

And who's going
to pay for that?

The bride's parents, of course.

Grarol hurried out of the shed, muttering.

Terrible idea . . .

-19-
Old Onions

Fatty and I are getting **NO** sleep because of Brittainee snoring like a big bald pig all night.

Oink   Snuffle

← My bed

. . . and when we FINALLY get back to sleep she starts showering, drying and tonging her hair

Please, Mum, can you put her in Jay's room?

Goodness no! She might . . . you know, she's got a crush on him!

Or downstairs with Grarol?

No! Mum would never stand for that — Brittainee calls her 'Grandma'.

You've got to admit she's awful, Mum.

I won't have it, Jelly! She's a perfectly nice girl.

I DON'T BELIEVE IT!

Brittainee had bought lots of delicious food and written her name on it all.

That selfish girl! She's happy to eat all our food and use all our hot water—

And our slippers.

122

Julian told us that he hadn't liked to say, but Brittainee had been wearing his slippers for several days.

Morning, Jay!

But Mum said we still had to be nice to her and show her a good time because her ~~mom~~ mum would think BAD things about us otherwise.

SO Fatty and I have moved into the shed temporarily until Brittainee leaves and I'm quite enjoying it — it's making me think about when I have my own flat. I have arranged everything exactly as I want it.

I've got a kettle 🫖 , a toaster 🍞, (toast whenever I want it without

Grarol informing me of the calorie content), a blow-up bed, bedside light, radio etc.

I enjoyed getting it all nice for the last Faithful Club meeting before the wedding. Myf and Roobs arrived and threw their coats on the floor and made themselves some toast, dropping crumbs everywhere. Then Ricky knocked all my ornaments off the shelf just by opening the door. They are making my flat look messy just by being in it! I swept up around them and made them hang their coats up and then started on the **agenda** for the meeting.

Right, number one on the agenda . . .
Myf, can you use a plate please?!

Sorree!

That's better, right . . . Firs . . . Ricky,
please can you stop runkling up that rug?

Gawd, Jelly, you sound like my mum!

Yes, well, I'm starting to feel quite
sympathetic towards her, Ricky.

Roobs said (with her mouth full),

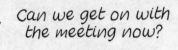

Can we get on with
the meeting now?

A crumb fell out of her
mouth on to the floor.

I tried to ignore it.

125

'Right, f-i-n-a-l-l-y,' I said.

'1. Fund for the O.M.G.! concert. Roobs, please give us the lowdown.'

'Right,' said Roobs. 'We made:

£27 from the beauty parlour, though we've had to refund Grarol £7.00 for her eyebrows after she went to the opticians to get new face furniture — I mean, *glasses.*

£6.30 from the Zoo.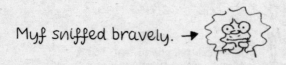

£1.77 saving on toast by buying cheaper bread and . . .

£2.01 saving on crisps by buying the cheaper ones.

£3.34 from Myf, who has kindly donated the money she was saving for a pet newt . . .'

Myf sniffed bravely. →

'Jelly and I made **£5** helping weed Alan and Dot next door's garden.'

Flash forward to next spring.......
Alan's bulbs (AKA 'old onions') have bloomed
in DICK's garden and won first prize in the
Boxford Gardens in Bloom competition.

and Myf has been selling her self-published
self-help book, *Tricks in Inoyation* . . .

TRICKS
IN
INOYATION

By
Myfanwy
Hughes

INDEX
1. How to deal with
   showoffs
2. An inoyer
3. How to deal with
   an inoyer
4+5. A double inoyer
   for a friend

If someone is
showing of be an
inoyer and ignore
them specially if
they have got new
clothes.
1.

If you want to
inoy somone who
has just washed
their hair or had it
cut, say your hair
looks dirty or your
hair needs cutting.
2.

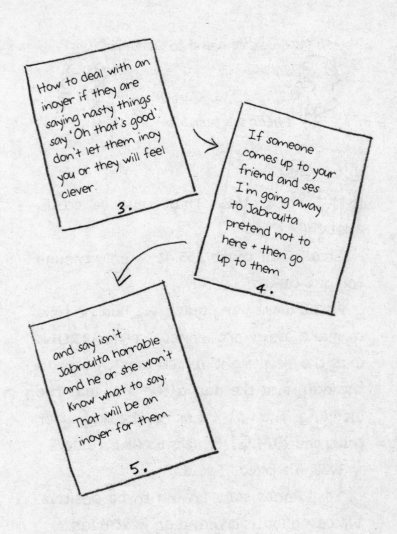

How to deal with an inoyer if they are saying nasty things say 'Oh that's good'. don't let them inoy you or they will feel clever.

3.

If someone comes up to your friend and ses I'm going away to Jabroulta pretend not to here + then go up to them

4.

and say isn't Jabroulta horrable and he or she won't Know what to say. That will be an inoyer for them.

5.

. . . even though it's all spelt wrong and is rubbish, it has been surprisingly popular and earned us £12 ⟶

So Dick, you're going to Gibraltar?

Yes, Alan, I . . .

I hear it's terrible.

Oh.

Myf cried, 'Yay! That must be easily enough!'

'So all in all, that's **£55.42** . . . only enough for one ticket.'

We all went very quiet. We had no time to make any more money. TOMORROW was the hen 'night' which was in fact in the day, and the day after that was the wedding. Then at 9 a.m. on the day after that, the **O.M.G.!** tickets went on sale.

'Well, we tried,' I said.

'Yes,' Roobs said, trying to be positive. 'We can always try and go next year.'

But Myf refused to believe it and decided to recount the money several times.

But however hard she tried, it never came to £200.

And she was making an appalling mess. Roobs was comfort-eating toast and Ricky and Fatty were playing ball and knocking everything off the shelves again. I had to order them all outside while I swept up and plumped up the cushions.

I'm starting to see why Mum is such a dictator after she's cleaned the kitchen floor and Hoovered everywhere (she

passes our dinner
through the cat flap
and we have to eat
outside).

It's a nightmare – I don't want my
own flat any more. I might just live in a
commune and hide when it's time for me
to do my chores. (Like I did when I was
living in the house. **Actually** I might as well
just move back there.)

Old Girls

It's 11 a.m. on the day of the hen and stag 'nights'. The hens are all gathered together waiting for Cousin Amelia to arrive. She has a very busy morning for an 8-year-old on a Saturday. Lessons in clarinet, ballet, tap, karate and Mandarin.

Shou shihua su ayi, wo bu xihuan zheyang de sanmingzhi*

(Bilingual in English and Body language)

Oh, I'm terribly sorry, would you like Jamie Oliver to come and make you one?

Pour être honnête, je préfère Michel Roux Junior.**

+?@£@! ***

* Mandarin translation: To be honest, Auntie Sue, I don't like this sandwich.
** French translation: To be honest, I'd prefer Michel Roux Junior.
*** Censored.

Brittainee is all dressed up. She even has a dressy brace covered in crystals on her teeth, and she keeps ÷flashing÷ it at Jay...

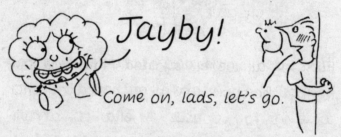

Jayby!

Come on, lads, let's go.

...who has never looked so KEEN to go tree hugging, though I can't help noticing he keeps going pink.

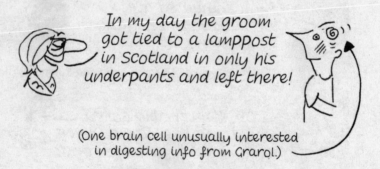

In my day the groom got tied to a lamppost in Scotland in only his underpants and left there!

(One brain cell unusually interested in digesting info from Grarol.)

As well as the diamond-effect brace, Brittainee has done her hair all...

BIG and BOUFFANT

It's because she thinks we're doing the 𝒫𝑜𝑠𝒽 things SHE suggested for the hen night — well we are, but on the cheap. On the VERY cheap.

First of all we blindfolded Mum and put her on the bus.

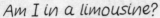

Am I in a limousine?

Ye-es.

Who's playing drum and bass and swearing?

Gee, funny-looking limo, so big and red! I didn't know you had so many friends, Sue!

Come on, girls, let's rock!

'Ere, who you calling a girl!?

Oooh! How exciting! I haven't been chased by men for years, what do they look like?

Aaaah!

Wa-it!

Then we got to the 'Hamburger joint' and Brittainee immediately cheered up.

Gee, Sue, you can take your blindfold off now!

It **IS** McDonald's! (Don't tell Julian!)

Brittainee had been in a **mood** all morning but McDonald's was the only place in Boxford, Europe she hadn't said **sucked**.

Then we did h<u>a</u>n<u>g</u>i<u>n</u>g o<u>u</u>t in the shopping centre which Mum *really* enjoyed because we spent too long in Claire's Accessories clogging up the pathways and not buying anything. The sales assistant said,

Come on, girls, if you're not going to buy anything you'll have to leave the shop.

She called me a girl!

An' me!

No, not you, Dot.

Brittainee had gone back in her 'this moll **SUCKS**' mood and Grarol had joined her now the relief at not having to pay for anything _posh_ had worn off.

Cousin Amelia missed this bit out.

Quia Verba Latina
mini cognoscere apis
orthograohium *

But she was back for the pool party doing
lengths because she had a swim meet the
next week.

Mum had a whale of a time and was **dead**
chuffed because she got called a girl again.

* Latin translation: I have to learn my verbs for my Latin
spelling bee.

Grarol and Brittainee sat on the edge complaining that their *hair* and **make-up** would run and get ruined.

Then it was back for DVDs and a sleepover in the shed. Brittainee insisted that we watch a gross-out movie • • •

Ha ha ha! Gross!

• • • that only she laughed at.

Then she fell asleep and we all went to sleep in my room because she was snoring so LOUDLY.

Snuffle
Oink

As we walked into the house, the stags were in the kitchen being very silly and trying on the bridesmaids' dresses, and Jay even had Mum's meringue on — Mum went berserk!

But not as berserk as she went when she realised that Julian wasn't among them.

Where is my husband-to-be?

Oh, Mum, it's really funny —
you'll really laugh!

Now I really am worried, because I know this isn't going to be funny.

 Well — he's tied — not tied exactly — he's attached — to a tree . . . in Epping Forest.

(losing confidence)

 Whaaaaaaaaaat???

He hugged this tree.

. . . he was tiddly . . .

. . . and his jumper got caught on it.

We might've slightly tied the sleeves together.

Hurr, hurr, hurr

I want you to point out roughly where he is.

Hurr hurr - there - hurr hurr.

And now we're going to get a search party together and go and rescue him.

Wha'?! It's dark!

Exactly – Julian will be terrified!

Brittainee had sloped in at that point, yawning.

Gee, Alan – that's my dress!!

While the rest of us gathered together torches and bottles of water, Jay ⁝SUDDENLY⁝ went very tired and a bit ill (his usual reaction to any kind of chore).

Come on, Jay! This is all your fault!

Oh, Mum, I feel sick . . .

'That search party idea **sucks**,' Brittainee said. 'I'll stay here with you, Jay. We can watch a date movie.'

Jay was up.

'Give me the map.'

'Is everything OK, Mrs Rowntree?'

It was Sandy, ⁝FRESH⁝ from a rehearsal in the garage.

Brittainee le**a**pt up.

'Oh Sandee! Julian's gone missing in a forest and we need to search for him.'

'Do you want me to help look for him,

Mrs Rowntree?' Sandy asked, smiling politely at Brittainee.

'Oh, yes please, Sandy, you're an angel.'

'I'll go in Sandy's team!' Brittainee cried. 'I bet he'll find Julian first.'

'Actually,' Jay said, snatching the map, 'I'm very good at orienteering.'

Brittainee flashed him a metallic *smile*, 'No you're not!'

'I am! I did it in Cubs.'

Everyone laughed. It was quite hard to take Jay seriously, especially when he was wearing Mum's wedding dress.

Mum suddenly noticed that someone had eaten a slice of the wedding cake.

Who did this?!

Jay went very *red*.

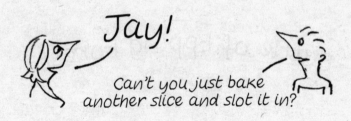

Jay!

Can't you just bake another slice and slot it in?

'Jay! You todal dork!' Brittainee screeched, and then cooed to Sandy, 'C'm'on Sandy, let's get in the car.'

Jay went **redder**, then a bit white with a tinge of green.

If I didn't know better I would've said he was a bit jealous of Brittainee's attentions towards Sandy. Maybe he was human after all and wanted Brittainee now she was unobtainable.

-21-
Battle of Epping Forest

THERE were two cars going to Epping Forest — Mum's, and Dot and Alan's.

Sandy hurried into the back of Dot's car, concerned about Julian. Brittainee **pushed** herself forward, concerned about sitting next to Sandy; I **pushed** into the seat the other side of Sandy, and Jay **pushed** into the seat the other side of Brittainee.

As we set off, mine and Sandy's knees were pressing together, which made it impossible to relax my leg and it felt like it was **quivering**.

(Concerned about Julian)

(Concerned about quivering leg)

But then he suddenly jerked his leg away and I felt all rejected. Don't be *silly*, I told myself, but as it was me saying it to me it didn't really help.

When we got to Epping Forest and to the tree that Julian had been 'attached' to, all that was left of him was some bits of 𝖜𝖔𝖔𝖑.

'Right, get into three small groups!' Mum shouted, holding back the tears. 'If we don't find him I will have to get married to a cardboard cut-out!'

← STIFF

I stood near Sandy (not **looking** at him, of course).

'OK, Sandy . . .' Mum began.

'Jelly wants to go with Sandy!' Myf yelled.

'I'm sure she doesn't,' Sandy laughed.

'No, I, er, ooh . . .' I stuttered.

'I wanna go with Sandy!' Brittainee shouted.

'Oh, well, I . . .' Sandy stammered.

'Me too!' Jay cried.

No, you're coming with me, young man!

'C'm'on, Sandy, let's go this way – it looks all private and dark!' Brittainee whispered to Sandy.

'Hold on a minute!' Myf called. 'We're coming with you, aren't we, Jells!'

The teams all going off in different directions to search for Julian were:

1. Me, Myf, Brittainee and Sandy.
2. Mum, Jay and Fatty.
3. Dot, Alan and Roobs.

In our group Brittainee was now pretending to be weedy and scared to get Sandy's attention.

Gee Sandy, you're so tall! How tall are you?!

This way, Sandy!

I had absolutely no personality because I was :paralysed: with nerves (I don't know why! I mean Sandy's got a **girlfriend**! Not that I would care if he didn't!).

Blank

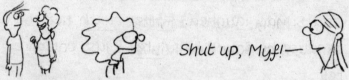

I don't know how to just go and get something I want. I'm "scared" I won't get it, so I don't bother.

Sandy was being VERY polite and gentlemanly so Myf became the leader — even *I* let her!

She kept saying:

And we all followed, Brittainee clinging on to Sandy and calling 'Julian!' in a silly high voice, with me bumping into trees and tripping over twigs trying to see what was going on. Was he just being polite, or did he *actually* *like* Brittainee???

I heard her say, 'This forest **sucks**,' and Sandy laughed. <u>At</u> her, <u>with</u> her, or because he found her <u>cute</u>? I just couldn't tell.

It was getting VERY dark and Brittainee kept pushing branches away and then thwacking them in my face.

Myf continued to lead us, shouting, 'This way!', 'Through this bush!', 'Down here!', 'Up here! Ooh.'

'What's this?' Brittainee demanded.

'A golf course!' I yelled. 'For crying out loud, Myf! Give me the map, you idiot! We've come *miles* the **WRONG** way!'

When I looked up from the map Brittainee and Sandy had ═disappeared.

Myf and I stood looking round . . . Myf started shouting,

Brittaineeee! Sandeeee! Not forgetting Juuulian!

'Shhh,' I told her, and pointed to a sandpit. Myf and I crept across the grass.

GOTCHA!

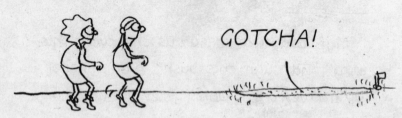

. . . we heard Brittainee say, 'I know you want me, Sandy.'

We looked down. She had managed to 'fall' into the sandpit with Sandy.

'Er . . .' Sandy said, trying to escape her clutches.

Hey! When I want something I get it, OK dude?!

'The thing is, Brittainee,' Sandy explained politely, 'you're a very . . . nice . . . girl, but I'm taken.'

'Too bad, I don't care if you've got a girlfriend.'

'I haven't got a girlfriend. But I like someone else. I like—'

'JELLEEEEEEEEEEE!'

Brittainee jumped out of her skin and fell backwards into the sand.

It was Julian S T A G G E R I N G towards the edge of the sandpit, his sleeves trailing about 20 metres behind him, calling.

'Jelleeee! Sandeeee! Myfanweeeee!' (and less enthusiastically), 'Brittaineee!'

Sandy stood up.

Sandeeee!

. . . Julian cried dramatically and threw his sleeves down into the sandpit to help Sandy up. We all gathered round Julian to see if he was OK.

'Hey!' Brittainee yelled. 'Whaddabout me?! He made me bite my lip!' she screeched, pointing up at Julian. 'What did he have to come along and spoil everything for?'

'But it's Julian we've been looking for,

Brittainee,' Sandy explained sweetly.

'Oh whadever!' she snarled,
spitting sand out of her mouth.

'Come on, Julian,' I said. 'Mum will be so
pleased we've found you!'

Just then, Mum and Fatty's silhouettes
appeared on the crest of the hill and Mum's
torch shone on Julian.

Julian!!! I'm going to kill you!

Well, we can still get married, but THEN I'm going to kill you!

The Bells Are Going to Chime!

The wedding morning arrived and Julian and Mum were bickering. Julian looked like he would much rather be **killed** than have to get married.

But I want a champagne breakfast in bed! It's traditional!

Please, Sue, your voice is so shrieky!

(Shriekily) It's because you had that half a lager and lime! You can't take your drink!

(groan)

Then there was a knock at the door. It was Mrs Vaughan.

'Oh, hello, Mrs Vaughan,' Mum said. 'I'm sorry but Neville and Whiskers are busy today.'

'No, it's Jelly I'm after.'

'Well,' Mum said nervously, imagining her Head Bridesmaid being kidnapped and renamed Tiddles . . .

Tiddles!

she's busy too.

'I just wanted to give her this. You see my daughter sold **lots** of my useful stuff at a car boot sale and I wanted Jelly and her friends to have **half** the proceeds, and a voucher for Neville for a week's stay at my newly re-opened Pet Boarding house. Anyway, give them my best, I've got to dash — I've got my first guests arriving this morning.'

Raaay!

Mum handed me an envelope with 'The Faithful Club' on it — it had **£153.16** in it! Exactly enough so that we could get our O.M.G.! tickets!!!!

I met Myf and Roobs in the shed where we had arranged to have our hair done by Brittainee, and broke the news. We all jumped around and screamed and kissed our **O.M.G.!** poster.

I calmed down after a bit and remembered it was my mum's wedding today. But Roobs and Myf continued to scream and dance about. They were EXTREMELY EXCITED about –

a) Us having hit our O.M.G.! ticket target of £200!
b) Being bridesmaids!
c) Just being alive!

I *was* excited about hitting our **O.M.G.!** ticket target, BUT I *wasn't* excited about being a bridesmaid/being alive

The fact that Sandy had said he
hadn't got a girlfriend but did like someone
was making me even more NERVOUS
about being a bridesmaid in front of him.

I'd been awake all night worrying. What
if it wasn't ME he liked? Or, even more
SCARY, what if it *was* me he liked?

Mum and Julian were getting married,
having the lunch and throwing the party all
in the same hotel, so So.M.G.! were playing
the R'n'B music for our street-dance
entrance as well as the cover versions
of Mum's playlist at the party – so NOW
Sandy was going to see me **NOT** being able
to street dance in my *Stupid* dress as
well as everything else . . .

(not that I cared, obviously).

ANYWAY, the tickets for **O.M.G.!** were going on sale the next morning so we made a plan to meet at Roobs' house at 8.30 a.m. where there were three available laptops

so we could all be online trying to get tickets at the same time.

Cousin Amelia turned up late having been at all her Sunday morning activities and Brittainee finally came stomping down the lawn still wearing Julian's slippers. ↗

   Brittainee spent an AGE on her own hair (at least three quarters of an hour).

We all looked forward to having the same hairdo and carefully applied **make-up**.

But when it got to us she was suddenly in a huge rush and just scraped our hair back all **tight** with elastic bands,

Ow!

and plonked some flowers on our heads. Then she smeared something brown and horrible on our faces, and tickled us with a 'bronzing brush'.

Hee, hee, hee!

Obviously, Amelia had done a kids' training course in hair and make-up at the BBC last summer and had done her own hair and make-up.

To be honest, I never let anyone
else do my hair and make-up.

You should,
sister.

When we complained, Brittainee said,

I can't help it if there's nothing to work with!

-23-
RUCKSACK of HOPE

Now we were properly late and by the time we got there we could hear the R'n'B music starting up and had to go straight into our 'routine'.

Myf stood on the threshold and went

A-one, a-two, a-one, two, three, four!!

and she started doing AMAZING back-flips and stuff down the aisle with Amelia doing her ballet and Brittainee behind **thinking** she was doing the same as Myf but actually just dancing about holding her hairdo in place, and then behind her me and Roobs doing an assortment of TERRIBLE moves, roll overs, semi-cartwheels and made-up jumping thingies.

The congregation had a jolly good laugh

Ha, ha, ha, ha, ha

and as I did an approximation of a backward roll diagonally into Uncle Frank's artificial leg I caught upside down eyes with Sandy. Because his face was upside down I couldn't tell if he was:

a) horrified
b) impressed.

But I was pleased I had my nether regions safely in those pants

Fortunately, Mum didn't notice any of this. Julian had **fainted**.

Julian! Get up!

Fatty had been patiently bearing the ring and hadn't eaten since his pre-nuptial diet Bonio.

But he was starting to get NERVOUS, and when he gets nervous he eats his back. Normally he would have been wearing his lampshade to stop him but Mum didn't think it was a good look for her Big Day. Suddenly, he could bear it no longer — he tried to eat his back and accidentally ate the wedding ring instead.

Mum screamed so loudly she roused Julian.

Fattaaaaay!
Give it back!!

Whaa'?

Julian loves a practical challenge. (much more than he loves a romantic occasion) . . . and while Mum was shaking Fatty, Julian fetched his all-purpose rucksack.

Julian's rucksack is a bit like the Room of Doom — which is a room in our house that's full of useless stuff. But rather than being large and having nothing of any use in it, Julian's Rucksack of Hope is small but has everything you could ever need in it:

166

Things in Julian's Rucksack of Hope

He L♥VES any opportunity to save the day with the contents of his rucksack. Sometimes Jay and I tease him.

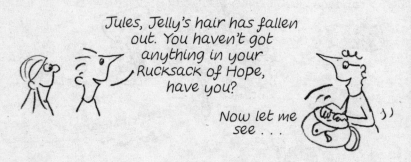

Jules, Jelly's hair has fallen out. You haven't got anything in your Rucksack of Hope, have you?

Now let me see . . .

How about this? Not quite Jelly's style but a good stop gap.

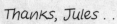

Thanks, Jules . . .

Or . . .
this hat?

ANYWAY, he fashioned Mum a new ring out of wire and stuck a barley sugar on it (Fatty ate it later). He was very chuffed as he is well into recycling.

-24-
A Todal Dork

Mum was very brave and during her speech at the lunch she said,

'The good thing about Fatty pooing in the house is we won't have any trouble retrieving my real ring!'

This made quite a lot of the guests gag on their Beef Wellington.

I was so relieved that the ceremony was over and that I wouldn't see Sandy till the party that nothing could spoil my GINORMOUS appetite.

I saw Jay was looking a bit white and sweaty when he stood up to do his speech and I was thoroughly looking forward to him making a complete *fool* of himself.

But he was hilarious! The guests were literally rolling around clutching their sides. It was like everyone had been given laughing gas — he was SO funny.

Unintentionally funny that is.

He talked utter gibberish with occasional moments of clarity which just made the gibberish even more funny.

GIBBERISH... Julian is a very good... um, step ladder, GIBBERISH... and I'm proud to call him my sister... GIBBERISH... I'm very much looking forward to being Jay Mildew. GIBBERISH... he came to live with us when he was 13 and... MORE GIBBERISH

But what really made it funny was he kept going UP and ▼

▲ D O W N in VOLUME.

And in the face of a hundred people with their mouths wide open guffawing and Brittainee shouting,

 ⸺ Oh Jay, you todal dork!!

his eyes went a bit watery and he said 'Brittainee! You're such a . . . complete cow!'

Then he flounced out of the room and several minutes later could be seen fleeing across the lawn and zig-zagging into the distant rhododendrons.

Only I was allowed to call Jay a ~~todal~~ total ~~dork~~ idiot! It's very hard to see your brother upset however much he deserves it.

I screeched out of my seat and went to go after him.

But I wasn't the only one.

Sandy Blatch, who knew a thing or two about people laughing at him and had witnessed the wHOLE thing from where he was setting up for the ⚬Diṣc̣o̤⚬, was already striding along the lawn calling after him.

And Brittainee was hot on Sandy's heels pretending to be concerned for Jay.

'Jayby! C'mon! Wait for me, Sand.'

As I trailed behind her I saw she was taking her brace out. Sandy stopped in front of her to look around – oh no! She was going to **kiss** him!

But Brittainee just kept right on going,

Jaaybyyy!
There he is!!
Jaybeeeey!

173

Jay came out from behind a rhododendron bush and started staggering away.

'Leave me alone!' he yelled dramatically. But Brittainee rugby tackled him to the ground, leapt on him and kissed him hard on the lips. And he didn't push her off either.

It was grotesque!!!!! (Or todally gross as Brittainee would say.)

The volume of laughter went UP ▲ and when I looked back towards the hotel everyone was **pressed** against the big glass windows still **roaring** with laughter at the sight of Jay trapped under Brittainee, her dress and hairdo.

'Very strange mating ritual,' Sandy said to me, laughing. I looked round at him just as . . .

GO ON JELLY!
WHY DON'T YOU
GIVE SANDY A
KISS TOO!

It was Myf screeching from the hotel.
Sandy laughed.

SHUDDUP, MYF!

I shouted, going **scarlet**.

'That's fine with me,' Sandy said.

I looked at Sandy, I was sure he was laughing at me and the words, 'Thanks but no thanks,' were on my lips just as I heard a distant cry of . . .

'B U U U N D A A A A L!!!!!'

and a crowd of wedding guests came galloping towards us and **le⍺pt** on top of Jay and Brittainee.

'Come on!' Sandy said.

And laughing we ran and jumped on top.

Though **squashed** by the guests, Jay had been a big hit and seemed unfazed by his encounter with Brittainee. In fact he was positively glowing.

Brittainee had done the being-obtainable-then-not-being-obtainable trick that Julian told me about.

Back in the ☼DISCO☼, So.M.G.! played 'Lady in Red' for the first dance. Mum and Julian were dancing, and Fatty was joining in, jumping up at them. Everyone was going 'Ah how $weet, look at the little doggy,' but I knew he was just trying to get at Mum's barley sugar ring.

THEN Jay and Brittainee joined them on the floor doing a (disgusting) slowie.

I just don't get it — what does he <u>see</u> in her?!!!

Mind you, what does she see in <u>him</u>, I s'pose.

After So.M.G.! had finished playing 'Lady in Red', they continued with Mum and Julian's playlist.

I danced with Myf
            Roobs
            Mum
            Julian
            Fatty

and tried to avoid **looKing** at Sandy cos I could FEEL him looking at me . . .

But when I finally braved a stare back over Myf's shoulder . . .

he wasn't looking at me, but smiling at Benji B. He obviously wasn't even remotely aware of me. I could've kicked myself (if it wasn't for my <u>stupid</u> long dress) for thinking he might still be interested.

-25-
Queen Myf

Myf is like the Queen. That may sound like an unlikely comparison, as obviously Myf is not old, posh, popular or rich. But she is like her in one subtle way.

They say the Queen thinks the world smells of FRESH paint because people have always just finished redecorating when she arrives for a visit.

Hello

Well Myf thinks the world is full of people who say shut up. She hears it so often she thinks it is a polite form of greeting. Consequently she takes no notice and continues to put her foot in it at full volume.

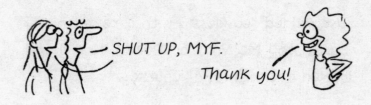

SHUT UP, MYF.

Thank you!

As we danced our fourth slowie to 'Everything You Do' by Bryan Adams, even though my ear was right next to her big gob and we were just swirling past Sandy Blatch on the keyboards and I was trying to look as graceful as you can with a mad midget treading on your feet – she shouted – yes, SHOUTED –

Look, Jelly! Sandy Blatch and his weirdo friend are STARING at us!!

Shut UP, Myf

MAYBE THEY DO FANCY US!!

– she continued at full volume. But luckily I don't think they heard her as they had

179

just melded seamlessly into a rendition of 'Don't Stop Me Now' by Queen. Not that I looked over , of course.

I spent the rest of the party doing the opposite of what I wanted to do, which was look over at Sandy Blatch. When I'd had my nano glance earlier I'd noticed how much he was looKing like Buster Bauble in his So.M.G.! persona.

When I did finally sneak another glance at the stage I was VERY disappointed to find that he and So.M.G.! were gone. Completely GONE!

They were such a good covers band that they sounded **exactly** like the playlist on Mum's iPod. But really I should've realised they were no longer playing when Benji

came and asked Myf to dance,

forcing me to dance with my Uncle with the artificial leg for the next four songs.

I had been waiting for SOMETHING to HAPPEN and now it was too late.

Then the lights came up and the wedding was over.

We all piled in to the minibus taxi and headed home for cups of tea. But when we got home something RATHER unfortunate had happened.

Honeymoon for One

We were all sitting around enjoying that lovely 'It's all over now we can relax' feeling, drinking hot tea and dunking biscuits, when suddenly there was a loud scream. Mum and Julian's passports had been left next to Hamwich's cage and he had dragged Julian's through the bars and shredded it to make a new nest.

They were supposed to be leaving the next morning for Greece.

Mum burst into tears.

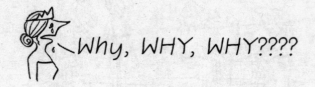

Why, WHY, WHY????

Oh, for goodness sake, Susan, why on earth did you leave the passports next to the rat's cage?

He's not a rat, is he, Jelly?

Shut UP, Mother! Can't you see I'm upset!

'Well your father and I just had a night in Skegness and back to work the next day,' Grarol informed us, adding, 'You could still go. Shame to waste the tickets.'

'I'm not going on honeymoon on my own!' Mum cried.

Julian put his arm round her, 'I REALLY don't mind, Susan, you'll probably have more fun without me there . . .'

She looked like she was considering it,

but then wailed,

'No! I want to go on honeymoon with my husband!!!'

Myf, Roobs and I caught each other's eyes.

-27-
The Eyes Have It

Myf, Roobs and I went straight to the shed to have a <u>secret</u> meeting. WE **HAD** been planning to stare at the **O.M.G.!** poster and giggle and talk about how excited we were about seeing them live. Roobs had put the £200 in her dad's account so we could pay with his card online at 9 a.m. the next day.

'But the agenda has changed,' Roobs said with utmost seriousness. 'We have enough to get a new honeymoon for your mum and Julian. I think we should have a vote.' She rang the bell.

'The question is, should we use our **O.M.G.!** money to buy a new honeymoon for Sue and Julian Mould? All those against, say nay.'

Myf's and my arms twitched violently with
the effort of keeping them down and we
literally had to press our lips together to
not say 'Nay'.

'All those in favour, say aye,' said Roobs.
She shouted 'Aye' and her arm shot up, but
mine and Myf's sort of fluttered into weak
teapot spout shapes around our shoulders,

and we croaked 'Aye' and nearly choked
on it. But then, NAY!!

a loud voice BOOMED in the doorway.

It was Ricky.

'Ricky!' Roobs admonished. 'Don't be so selfish!'

I couldn't help it. It just came out. I really want to see O.M.G.!

'So what did you mean to say?' Roobs asked him, in her best head teacher-ish voice. Ricky ~~blushed~~ and looked at his feet.

Aye.

'The ayes have it!' Roobs pronounced.

We **snuck** up to Julian's computer and went online to look for last minute holiday deals. Myf didn't quite understand the passport thing . . .

What about Tenerife?!

But Roobs got on the phone to her dad who suggested Center Parcs and we found a last minute deal at the Sherwood Forest one. We paid for it and printed out the details then went and presented it to Mum and Julian.

The screaming was **DEAFENING**.

Aerial tree trekking!

World of Spa! Dedicated to pampering!

Julian insisted on a group *hug* which was quite SCARY . . .

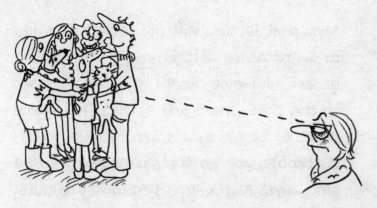

Grarol looked a little shame-faced (even with her permanent **arched** eyebrow) and said,

'Oh. That's so generous of you, girls, and you've forsaken going to see your favourite band?'

'It's called selflessness, Mother.'

'Is it? I see . . .' she said, thoughtfully. 'And how much are these tickets to see Oh My God!?'

'£40 each including booking fee and £10 for the coach ticket,' Roobs told her.

'Hmm,' said Grarol, tapping on her gold plated calculator.

Mum and Julian went off to bed, and Jay and Brittainee settled down to watch a gross-out movie, Roobs, Myf and I went to the shed where we were spending the night to giggle and stare at our O.M.G.! poster (Buster Bauble was looKing extra like Sandy Blatch, and I tried not to think about how I messed up again) — it was OBVIOUS Grarol was going to get us O.M.G.! tickets!!!!!

A Twinge of Excitement

The next morning, we over-slept and it was 9.37 a.m. and we leapt up and rushed into the kitchen. Mum and Julian had already left for Sherwood Forest and Grarol was making breakfast — the only downside of Mum going away was Grarol was staying and was giving us grapefruit segments for breakfast. We didn't mind though because she said immediately:

'I have a surprise for you, girls! I thought what a selfish Gra- Grarol I am, and how I should do a selfless act like you did SO . . .'

We all started quaking with excitement as she got out an envelope . . .

'I have booked something for you I know you will l ❤ ve! . . . Well, open it!'

I tore it open . . . we looked at it . . . it didn't look like **O.M.G.!** tickets, or even a receipt for **O.M.G.!** tickets. It was a scrap of paper – with a picture of So.M.G.! on it – a sort of flyer.

'I don't understand, Grarol.'

'Well, the covers band that played for free last night at the wedding – they are actually an **O.M.G.!** tribute band!' she said triumphantly.

'Yes, Grarol, we know,' Myf said, unable to keep the sarcasm out of her voice.

'Well, aren't you excited?! I've arranged for them to come and give a concert for you and all your friends in the garden tonight!'

'Oh,' Roobs said.

I tried to look *disappointed* , but I was
secretly quite excited. That meant Sandy
was coming round and I would have an
excuse to stare at him and giggle without
looking too obvious. Myf as usual said
what I was thinking.

'Ooh, actually that's quite exciting,
because I reckon that Benji Whatsit fancies
me which means I now fancy *him* and I
get to hang out with him again!'

It was a lovely sunny evening and we had
called all our friends who
were O.M.G.! fans (Ricky and
Dot). We also asked Mrs V
round to say thank
you for the money and even
included Jay and Brittainee, who
were both being much nicer since
they had got together. Brittainee
had even bought Julian some new
slippers for his honeymoon.

We arranged blankets  and cushions on the grass and cold drinks and some crisps and chocolate which we paid for with our remaining £20.

The sun was setting by the time So.M.G.! started playing under the apple tree, and they played acoustic so it wasn't too noisy. Sandy played a glockenspiel instead of keyboards and they did all the hits, especially the soppy ones in a really nice soft summery way.

Even Benji was laid back though he did start laughing when Myf waved her scarf that had said 'Buster' but now said 'Benji' on it.

If we closed our eyes 👁 😑 👁 it was just like being at the real concert (except without all the screaming girls 👧 👧 👧) and if I opened my eyes it was still like being at the real concert because Sandy really did look like Buster Bauble (except he smiled and winked at me which I knew Buster *probably* wouldn't do and I could look at him and smile back because it would be rude not to when he was playing a free concert).

✨ 🌙 Afterwards we all sat under the stars ✨ and ate pizza that Grarol had made — she even let Fatty have a slice — and we all talked about the wedding and everything that had happened and it all started to seem funny now. Sandy said, 'Bundling Jay and Brittainee with you was the best bit, Jelly,' and we both giggled.

Then I lay on my back and Sandy lay beside me.

I could feel him staring at the side of my head, but I didn't feel any need to tuck my ears in. Insults can stay with you for years, but so can compliments, and I knew I would last quite a long time on 'cute ears'.

I pretended not to be interested when he started telling me in a low voice why he wasn't going out with Angel Farraday any more. He said it was because she had gone to a music academy for gifted triangle players. My cute ears pricked up when he said in an even lower voice, 'But the real reason I'm not going out with her any more is the same reason you wouldn't go out with me . . . because she was too short.' I spluttered with laughter at this – which made it quite hard to look like I wasn't interested.

I looked around at my lovely friends. Myf was laughing with Benji, Roobs was being given a maraca lesson by Callum, and Ricky was tickling

←Slightly more handsome than the real O.M.G.! drummer Jaz Jenkins

Fatty's tummy. Suddenly, I was rather looking forward to being Jelly Mould and felt a little twinge of excitement in my tummy about the future.

My Early Publishing Days

Myf's self-help book was based on my first published book (published by me!). It was quickly followed by *How to Embariss Your Friends* and the *How to Be Cleva Quiz Book*.

Sadly they are now out of print and not available in any good bookshops.

Here is a rare first edition of *Tricks in Inoyation*:

INDEX
1. how to
deal with show
offs
2. an inoyer
3. how to deal
with an inoyer
4. its a double
inoyer for
a freind.

1

If someone
is showing
of be an
inoyer and
ignore them
specially if
they have
got new
clothes

2

If you want
to inoy somone
who has
Just washed
their hair
or had it
cut say your
hair looks dirty
or your hair
needs cutting

3

how to deal
with an
inoyer if they
are saying nasty
things say
oh thats good
dont let them
inoy you or they
will feel
clever

4

If somone
comes up to
your and no
seak freind
and ses I'm
going away to
Jabroulta
and pretend Not
to here and
then go up

5

and
say isnt
Jabroulta
horrible and
he or she
wont no what
to say.

tha will
be an inoyer
bok them

Thank Yous

Thank you to the team at Macmillan – Rachel Petty, Helen Bray, Rachel Vale, Fliss Stevens – and especially Tracey Ridgewell, who goes beyond the call of duty doing the fiddly job of putting the pictures and words together and who is always chirpy and kind.

Thank you, as always, to my agent Veronique Baxter for listening and feeding me cappuccinos.

Plus a special thanks to Matthew Harding, who came up with the name 'So.M.G.!' for the O.M.G.! tribute band.

And last but not least, thank you to my mum for letting me have so many pets, and yet drawing the line at a kangaroo even though I had already designed the enclosure.